Adam's Daycare

**Story by
Julie Ovenell-Carter**

**Illustrations by
Ruth Ohi**

Annick Press • Toronto • New York

When Adam's mommy goes to work, Adam comes to Ina's house.

Ina helps him wiggle off his boots, and hangs his raincoat on a hook. Adam's mom kneels down for a goodbye hug, and Adam covers her face with kisses. Ina lifts Adam to the window, and he waves and waves, until he can't see his mother's car any more.

Then he runs upstairs to find his friends.

Adam and Anna like to build. They make castles out of cushions. They make boats out of boxes. Today, they are making a fire engine with the little red table and chairs. They are going to rescue Ina's dog from a burning building.

But when they get there, Ina's dog
is asleep, so they save Ina instead.

When Molly comes to Ina's house, Adam and Anna run to say hello. Today is Molly's birthday, and she is carrying a small white box. Adam and Anna try to guess what is inside, but Molly says it's a surprise. In the kitchen, Ina peeks: she counts five cupcakes with pink icing and yellow sparkles.

Molly and Adam are making crowns. Adam dips long green feathers in glue and puts one feather on each point. Molly sprinkles glitter all over her crown. Some sticks on her cheeks, like tiny golden freckles.

After a while the rain stops, and Ina asks the children to help her mail some letters. They lay their coats on the floor and flip them over their heads, the way Ina taught them. They pull on their boots.

On the way to the mailbox, Molly and Anna look for slugs. Molly finds a fat green slug with yellow splotches down its back. Anna finds a small black slug, skinny as her baby finger.

Everyone drops a letter through the slot, and then they all walk back to Ina's house, taking care to step in all the puddles.

Ina calls *Lunchtime!*, and Adam and Anna are first in line to wash their hands.

For dessert, Ina brings out the cupcakes and they all sing *Happy Birthday* to Molly. Then Anna accidentally tips her plate.

Her cupcake drops to the floor, and Ina's dog gulps it down. Anna starts to cry. Adam breaks his cake in half and shares it with Anna.

Adam, says Ina, has a very big heart.

After lunch, Adam bakes sandpies
with Molly in the backyard. Anna
gathers dandelions in a teapot for the
playhouse. Adam finds a worm in
the sandbox, and shows it to Ina.
He puts it back in the flower garden,
and watches it wriggle into the dirt.

Then he races Molly and Anna to
the top of the climbing-bars.

When the drizzly rain starts again, Ina calls
the children in for a story. Molly strokes her
ear and sucks her thumb and falls asleep,
cosy under Ina's blanket of words.

Anna's mom is first to come. She
carries Anna into the backyard to
admire her potful of dandelions, and
when they go, Adam sees she is
wearing some of the yellow flowers
in her hair.

At snacktime, Molly gets mad at
Adam for drinking all her apple
juice and is thinking about throwing
a piece of railway track when she
hears her daddy's truck, and starts
to smile.

Molly's daddy waits while
Molly finishes her popcorn,
and when they go, Adam
sees he is wearing Molly's
golden crown.

Later, Ina watches Adam watching cars pass by the window, waiting for the one he knows the best: only one headlight, but brand-new windshield wipers that don't smear the rain.

And then Adam's on his mommy like a little baby monkey, even though her coat is cold and wet. Say goodbye now, says his momma, time to go. Ina helps Adam wiggle on his boots, and zip up his raincoat.

Through the car window Adam waves and waves, until he can't see Ina's house any more.

*To Fiona Beaty, the Daycare Diva, and all
the little bantams, and
to Sandra Murray, with gratitude*

—J.O-C.

To Taavo

—R.O.

Annick Press Ltd. **All rights reserved**. No part of this work covered by the copyrights hereon may be reproduced or used in
any form or by any means – graphic, electronic, or mechanical – without the prior written permission of the publisher.

Annick Press gratefully acknowledges the support of the Canada Council and the Ontario Arts Council.

Cataloguing in Publication Data

Ovenell-Carter, Julie
Adam's daycare

ISBN 1-55037-445-1 (bound) ISBN 1-55037-444-3 (pbk.)

I. Ohi, Ruth. II. Title.

PS8579.V46A82 1997 jC813'.54   C97-930384-2
PZ7.O945Ad 1997

Distributed in Canada by:
Firefly Books Ltd.
3680 Victoria Park Avenue
Willowdale, ON M2H 3K1

Published in the U.S.A. by Annick Press (U.S.) Ltd.
Distributed in the U.S.A. by Firefly Books (U.S.) Inc.
P.O. Box 1338, Ellicott Station
Buffalo, NY 14205

Printed and bound in Canada.